OxyContin Abuse

Suzanne Slade

rosen publishing's

rosen central®

New York

To Officer Cybulski and all the other D.A.R.E. officers, in recognition of your tireless efforts in the fight against teenage drug abuse

Published in 2008 by The Rosen Publishing Group, Inc.
29 East 21st Street, New York, NY 10010

First Edition

Library of Congress Cataloging-in-Publication Data

Slade, Suzanne.
OxyContin abuse / Suzanne Slade.
    p. cm. — (Incredibly disgusting drugs)
Includes bibliographical references and index.
ISBN-13: 978-1-4042-1954-0
ISBN-10: 1-4042-1954-4
1. Oxycodone abuse—Juvenile literature. 2. Oxycodone—Juvenile literature. 3. Drug abuse—Juvenile literature. 4. Drugs—Juvenile literature. I. Title.
HV5822.O99S53 2008
613.8'3—dc22
                                                                    2007001028

Manufactured in The United States of America

Contents

Introduction

Have you ever heard of a pain medicine called OxyContin? OxyContin is the brand name for a prescription medication that helps people manage severe pain. But if people abuse OxyContin, this seemingly miraculous pain pill can create dependency, bring about slow breathing, or even cause death. People abuse this powerful drug when they use pills that are not prescribed for them. Abuse also occurs when patients take a higher dose of OxyContin than their doctor prescribes. OxyContin is available in tablets and capsules. Once swallowed, both are designed to slowly release medicine that helps get rid of pain. Many users crush the pills and swallow or inhale the powder, or mix the powder with water so that they can inject it into their bodies. By abusing the drug in these ways, users hope to create a powerful high.

When a large amount of OxyContin is suddenly introduced into the human body, instead of being released slowly into the bloodstream as intended by the painkiller's manufacturer, serious consequences can occur. As this dangerous drug courses throughout the body, it can cause unpredictable and damaging effects wherever it goes. The user's thinking becomes cloudy, and he or she is easily confused. The pupils in the user's eyes shrink, and vision is impaired. The person feels nauseated and often cannot stop vomiting. His or her skin turns cold and clammy, and muscles in the body become weak. The person may feel drowsy, suddenly lose consciousness, or experience frightening hallucinations. Breathing becomes difficult, and the respiratory system can shut down entirely. Depressed, or slowed down, breathing is a common cause of death for OxyContin abusers. The lethal effects of this drug come upon a user very quickly. There often isn't time to get medical help for someone who is struggling for every breath. Many OxyContin abusers die while their friends stand by helplessly. Other serious physical and behavioral symptoms of abuse include dizziness, constipation, dry mouth, severe headaches, mood changes, and loss of interest in social activities.

Doctors prescribe OxyContin to help their patients manage intense or ongoing pain. People with cancer may be given this drug. Cancer cells can multiply quickly and create large tumors. Tumors may press on nerve endings or blood vessels and become a source of severe pain. Cancer treatments help shrink tumors, but the treatments can take weeks or even months before patients feel relief from pain. OxyContin helps people who suffer with cancer deal with the pain their life-threatening disease causes. People with serious injuries also benefit from OxyContin.

Workers who have had accidents may need pain relief for broken bones or a major injury so they can sleep at night or go back to work. Ongoing back problems or back surgery can cause pain that may require a strong medicine such as OxyContin.

People should use OxyContin only if it has been prescribed specifically for them by a doctor. Doctors know the side effects of every drug and whether those side effects might be dangerous for certain patients, especially if they are taking other medications or drinking alcohol. Some drugs, like OxyContin, are very addictive. Doctors are careful to prescribe addictive medicines only when they are absolutely needed by their patients and doctors warn their patients of the risks associated with using the medications. Abuse of prescription drugs has dangerous and deadly consequences.

1
What Is
OxyContin?

OxyContin is the brand name of a prescription drug that relieves pain. It is manufactured by Purdue Pharma L.P. OxyContin has been made in five different strengths, each containing a different amount of the main ingredient, oxycodone. This ingredient's full name appears as oxycodone hydrochloride on the packaging. A chemist might use its chemical name, 14-hydroxydihydrocodeinone hydrochloride. This name is based on the elements in one molecule of oxycodone hydrochloride. The chemical name is quite a mouthful, so most people use the name oxycodone.

History of Oxycodone and OxyContin

Oxycodone was created in Germany in the early 1900s. People in Europe began using it to relieve pain in 1917. When oxycodone was first developed, it seemed this new miracle drug might solve the problems of other

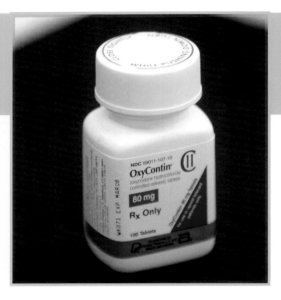

This bottle contains prescription pain-relieving pills called OxyContin. The childproof cap helps keep young children safe from this powerful drug.

pain-relieving drugs. Initial studies showed that it did not appear to be addictive, and it was effective against severe pain.

In the 1950s, people in America began mixing oxycodone with non-prescription pain medicines to create new and useful drugs. Since the 1960s, oxycodone has been used in more than fifty different prescription medications for pain. Two of the most commonly prescribed, in recent years, are Percodan and Percocet. Percodan is a mixture of oxycodone and aspirin. Percocet contains oxycodone and acetaminophen. Percocet and Percodan each contain 5 mg of oxycodone. Both mixtures provide fast pain relief because the human body can absorb the active agent, oxycodone, quickly. Although the pain-relieving effects of Percocet and Percodan are very effective, the relief doesn't last long. Patients must take several pills each day for continued pain relief.

In 1995, a new pill containing oxycodone, called OxyContin, became available. OxyContin slowly releases oxycodone over a twelve-hour time period. By taking two pills per day, a patient can receive pain relief for twenty-four hours. Although doctors in the United States have been prescribing this drug only since December 1995, it is already well known and widely used. In a few short years, OxyContin has replaced other popular pain drugs because it produces fewer side effects. OxyContin is often given to patients who have medical conditions that create severe or ongoing pain, such as cancer, a serious back injury, or arthritis. It usually is not prescribed for short-term health problems.

Identifying OxyContin

Each of the four OxyContin pills is a different color and size, but they all have the letters oc stamped on one side. The round tablets contain 10, 20, 40, or 80 milligrams (mg) of oxycodone. The 10 mg pill is white and is the smallest. The 20 mg strength is slightly larger and is pink. The 40 mg yellow pill is a little bigger. The largest round tablet is green and contains an 80 mg dose. The blue oval-shaped capsule contains 160 mg of oxycondone. (However, the manufacturer stopped shipping this high-dose pill

LOSE-UP VIEWS OF THE 20 MG AND 80 MG ⅔XY ONTIN TABLETS SHOW THE LETTERS ⅔ ON ONE SIDE; ⅔ STANDS FOR ⅔XY ONTIN.

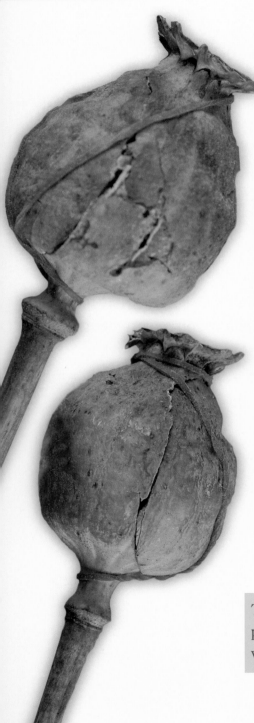

in 2001.) OxyContin pills have a thin coating that keeps them from breaking apart and makes them easier to swallow. Once swallowed, the thin coating is dissolved by stomach acid, allowing the pill to begin releasing its pain medication. OxyContin belongs to a class of prescription drugs called opioids, which help relieve pain.

The term "opioid" refers to substances that contain material from the opium poppy plant. People have been using opium poppies for thousands of years for their pleasurable and sleep-inducing effects. Historical records indicate that people first began using opium poppies in 3400 BCE. Some used it to treat stomach problems, poor eyesight, and asthma. While early opium poppy users did not understand the science behind their discovery,

The opium inside these poppy pods contains powerful ingredients such as codeine and morphine, which are used to make opioids.

Poppy Patrol

In 1942, the United States passed the Opium Poppy Control Act and banned people in America from growing the opium poppy plant.

they did know these beautiful pink and white flowers contained something powerful.

Today, scientists know much more about the pain-relieving ingredients hidden inside the poppy. This plant has been given the scientific name *Papaver somniferum*. It commonly is referred to as the opium poppy, after the powerful substance called opium that is extracted from its seed pods. Opium contains raw materials, such as codeine, noscapine, papaverine, thebaine, and morphine, which are used to make many opioids. For example, morphine is used to make a dangerous and addictive street drug called heroin.

There are several different types of opioids. Some natural opioids are made from poppy ingredients, while others are naturally produced in the human body. Synthetic opioids are produced by chemists and contain no natural ingredients. Methadone and fentanyl are examples of synthetic opioids. The third type of opioid is semisynthetic. These are created by combining natural opioid ingredients with synthetic ones. OxyContin is a semisynthetic opioid. It contains thebaine from poppies and synthetic chemicals.

How Drugs Block Pain

Over the years, scientists have made important discoveries about how opioid drugs block pain. First, this drug moves through a person's body in the bloodstream. Once the drug arrives at the brain and spinal cord, opioids attach to specific proteins called opioid receptors. Opioid receptors are large protein molecules that can affect our perception of pain. There are three types of receptors: mu, delta, and kappa. By attaching to opioid receptors, this drug stops pain messages sent from various parts of the body from reaching the brain. Even though the body may have an illness or injury that is creating intense pain, the brain does not receive these messages and the person will not feel pain.

Why OxyContin Was Developed

To understand why OxyContin was developed, it's important to know the history of other pain-relieving drugs. Americans frequently use over-the-counter pain medications for everyday pain. The phrase "over-the-counter" means a medicine you can buy without a prescription. Aspirin and acetaminophen (which is sold under the brand name Tylenol) are two common over-the-counter pain medicines. These are effective in treating minor or temporary pain but are sometimes not very successful in helping people

Abusing OxyContin, including injecting it, can lead to tragic results such as addiction, serious health problems, or even death.

with intense, long-lasting pain. If people with ongoing pain take several over-the-counter pills each day for long periods of time, they run the risk of creating new health problems. Even nonprescription pills can damage important organs such as the stomach or kidneys if a person takes too many.

As a result of the inability of nonprescription pain medicines to help with ongoing or severe pain, researchers began to develop more powerful, longer-lasting drugs. Some of the drugs they created, such as codeine and morphine, were quite effective, but they were extremely addictive also. People who took these drugs for an extended period of time experienced symptoms of withdrawal when they stopped taking them.

Proper Use

OxyContin must be used properly to help patients and keep them safe. OxyContin tablets are to be swallowed whole and should never be crushed or broken. This pill is designed to release oxycodone slowly over time. If a tablet is broken, too much of this drug will be released into the body and serious problems can arise. OxyContin is an adult medicine and is not approved for use by those under age eighteen. The drug's manufacturer lists this warning inside its packaging: "Safety and effectiveness of OxyContin has not been established in pediatric patients below the age of 18." Patients who are given OxyContin must keep this medicine locked up where others cannot get at it. An accidental dose could result in death. All prescription medicine, including OxyContin, should be taken only by the person for whom it was prescribed.

2
Effects
on the Body

cientists cannot fully explain what pain is or its cause. They do know the sensations people perceive as pain are processed in the brain. Skin and other tissues in the body send messages to the spinal cord along peripheral nerves. These messages are processed in the spinal cord and then sent to the brain. Although researchers are still learning and debating about the body's exact mechanisms of pain, most people would agree they prefer to avoid pain if possible.

Dangers to Your Body

OxyContin was designed to slowly release oxycodone over twelve hours. Abusers find ways to put a large amount of this powerful drug into their system at one time in an attempt to create a sudden feeling of euphoria. Some swallow several pills at once. Others may chew a pill so their body will quickly absorb all the active ingredients. Abusers often crush pills and snort the powder. Desperate for a high, some people crush a pill into a fine powder and dissolve it with water so they can inject this dangerous solution into their body with a needle. Many addicts reuse dirty needles or share them with others. This often leads to infectious, seeping wounds, or gangrene. Some users become seriously ill from these uncontrolled infections that attack their whole system. By sharing needles, OxyContin abusers also run the risk of exposing themselves to other life-threatening diseases such as HIV or hepatitis.

The Body Reacts

When the body is suddenly bombarded by high levels of oxycodone, any number of devastating results can occur. Drowsiness, constipation, nausea, dizziness, vomiting, headache, dry mouth, sweating, and weakness are all caused by too much oxycodone in the body. The effect of abusing this drug is completely unpredictable. An OxyContin overdose can make the body go into shock. In this state, the bloodstream is not able to provide enough nutrients to the body's cells and many cells starve. Too much oxycodone also can cause the circulatory system to stop working properly. Blood pressure will drop. Blood that carries oxygen and other vital nutrients throughout the body will be slowed, and organs will not receive their normal deliveries from the blood and may not function properly. In some cases, precious organs become permanently damaged.

While many parts of the body struggle against the sinister effects of the invading oxycodone, the respiratory system fights a battle of its own.

Severe nausea and uncontrolled vomiting are two of the many ways your body may react to an overdose of oxycodone, the active ingredient in OxyContin.

Large amounts of this drug can make breathing very difficult. In many instances, abusers experience respiratory arrest. This occurs when the respiratory system fails and a person's heart may stop because it is not receiving enough oxygen. The undeniable fact is that abusing OxyContin can kill. It *has* killed—teens, girls, boys, moms, and dads. It can very easily kill anyone who abuses it, even you.

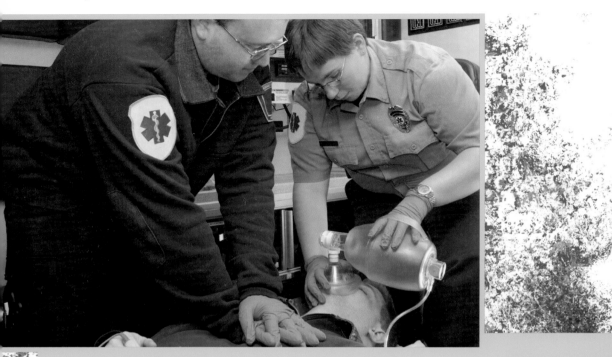

Even highly trained paramedics cannot always save an OxyContin abuser who has gone into respiratory arrest.

Dependency and Addiction

People who abuse OxyContin to get a high or euphoric rush soon find that they require more of this dangerous drug to get the same effect. Over time, the human body develops a tolerance to this drug, so higher doses are needed to achieve the same high as when a person first used it. Many users continue to need increasingly larger amounts of OxyContin as they attempt to re-create, or chase, their first high. Taking greater

A Deadly Game

The word "pharming" refers to a dangerous game that some teenagers play at parties. They bring prescription pills they have stolen from their parents and mix them together in a bowl. To play, each teen randomly swallows a few pills from the bowl. Some teenagers attending pharm parties trade their pills for ones others have brought. Popping a mixture of unknown pills can result in seizures or temporary breathing problems that may cause permanent brain damage. Some young adults have died by playing this deadly game just once.

doses of OxyContin increases the chance that serious side effects or even death will occur.

If a person continues to use and abuse powerful drugs, he or she may end up in a terrifying state called dependence. Dependence occurs when the body has adapted to the presence of a certain drug. When people become dependent on a drug, they are physically unable to stop taking it. Their bodies will have horrible side effects, called withdrawal symptoms, if they don't use the drug. It is a helpless feeling when a person realizes he or she cannot stop taking a harmful drug.

While drug dependency is a physical dependence on a certain drug, there is another condition many users fall into: drug addiction. Addiction is when a person is unable to stop abusing a drug for psychological reasons. Addicts cannot change their destructive habits, even after learning about the dangers of abusing drugs. Researchers have determined that addiction is a disease in which brain function has been changed due to substance abuse. Once people become addicted to a drug, the way they think is altered. Their top priorities in life become dangerously rearranged. An addict's mind cannot make rational or safe decisions and is ultimately motivated by the need to get more drugs. The drives behind addiction are very strong, and people usually require intensive help from professionals to successfully fight addiction.

People who become dependent or addicted to a drug are constantly worried about keeping a supply on hand. Many resort to stealing money or valuable goods that they can sell in order to buy more drugs. Some users become so desperate, they break into pharmacies and steal pills to get their next fix of OxyContin. Drug dependency and addiction lead to a hopeless way of life.

Mixing OxyContin and Other Drugs

Taking OxyContin along with other kinds of drugs or alcohol often has deadly results. It's impossible to know how vital organs and systems of the human body will react when they are assaulted by a mixture of drugs, each with its own side effects and warnings. Most prescriptions carry warning labels to alert patients of the risks associated with drinking

Some OxyContin abusers become so desperate that they resort to stealing electronic devices, such as digital cameras, to trade or sell for more pills.

alcohol when taking certain medications. One of the biggest dangers with OxyContin abuse is slowed or stopped breathing. Combining OxyContin with other substances increases the possibility of respiratory failure and death. In particular, medicines that cause drowsiness can interact with OxyContin and cause dizziness or severe sedation. Some of these medications include sleeping pills, tranquilizers, antidepressants, muscle relaxants, and seizure or anxiety medications. People with certain health conditions or diseases, such as asthma, hypothyroidism, Addison's disease, and liver or gall bladder disease, have a greater risk for serious health consequences or death if they take OxyContin.

Some addicts make the mistake of assuming that because they have abused OxyContin in the past, or they have mixed OxyContin with other drugs and survived, it's OK to take it with drugs or alcohol again. A person can die from abusing OxyContin just one time, even if he or she has abused it in the past. This drug can be fatal when taken by itself or when it is mixed with other drugs or alcohol. It can kill anyone at anytime and anywhere.

Precious organs can become permanently damaged, like this liver, by abusing OxyContin.

3

Effects
on the Mind

Some people are tempted to try OxyContin to obtain the brief feeling of euphoria, or high, that they believe they will experience. But when this short high ends, feelings of remorse and hopelessness often fill their minds. If a person continues to use drugs, he or she can become desperate for the next high and feel trapped by this need. Over time, helplessness sets in. Things that used to be bright spots in the user's life, such as hanging out with friends, playing sports, and spending time with family, become dim in the dark cloud of drug abuse. Taking OxyContin may lead to depression and thoughts of suicide. This drug often leaves its users asking, "Where is the happiness this tiny pill promised?"

OxyContin and Your Brain

OxyContin not only influences physical aspects of the body and relieves pain, but it also has the power to

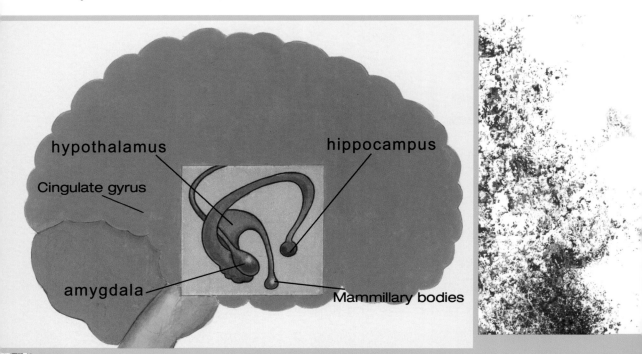

hypothalamus

hippocampus

Cingulate gyrus

amygdala

Mammillary bodies

Your brain is the control center of your body. OxyContin can "hijack" the brain and alter crucial functions within the limbic system.

alter emotions. OxyContin affects a person's mind and emotions when it travels through the bloodstream and enters the body's main control center, the brain. A human brain is made up of three main sections: the forebrain, midbrain, and hindbrain. Each section is responsible for several tasks.

The limbic system, the part of the brain that controls emotions, is located in the forebrain. Four structures—the amygdala, hippocampus, mammillary bodies, and cingulate gyrus—make up the limbic system. These areas direct the type of emotional response a person will have in different situations. Pain medications affect the limbic system and cause most people to experience a temporary sense of calmness or euphoria. While these feelings may attract some people to use OxyContin, most are unaware of the serious consequences this drug can have.

The limbic system also tells a person when he or she needs certain things that keep him or her alive, such as food, drink, or social relationships. High levels of OxyContin can take over the limbic system, creating an urgent craving for more of this drug. This craving can override the normal desires for essentials like eating a meal or spending time with friends. The frightening aspect of this drug is that the user is generally unaware that it is controlling his or her thoughts and desires.

Drugs and Decisions

When people take a drug that changes their emotions, they are altering their ability to make reasonable decisions. If normal judgment is impaired, bad results are sure to follow. People who are abusing OxyContin will find that their priorities become imbalanced. They may neglect family and their close friends. Studying or doing homework may seem unimportant in their new state of mind, and in time their grades will suffer. Future dreams of college or a job may suddenly seem impossible. A person who abuses OxyContin often forgets about healthy activities. Exercise and eating meals with the family are commonly ignored. Without nutritious food and exercise, a user's health will gradually slip away. A teenager who is losing friends, is doing poorly in school, feels sick most of the time, and sees little hope for the future may not even realize that drug use is the cause of his or her poor decisions and seemingly hopeless situation.

Use It or Lose It

A teenager's brain is about 95 percent of its future adult size of three pounds (1.4 kilograms). During puberty, a brain undergoes tremendous internal changes and growth that will determine its functioning capacity in later years. These changes are preparing a person's brain for the adult years ahead. Although a young teen's brain doesn't significantly change in size, it is building connections that will help it to organize, plan, and make decisions better. These connections are similar to the complex wire connections in a computer that allow it to function properly.

Early in life, a human brain creates many more connections than it will need. As the brain goes through normal development, it will begin to prune, or cut away, the connections that are not used. Much of this crucial pruning occurs in the early teen years. If a teen is actively learning and trying new activities, many of these connections will remain intact. But if a person decides to abuse harmful drugs, precious connections and brain cells are lost forever. Teens who take drugs like OxyContin are not only putting their immediate health at risk, but they also are throwing away their own potential thinking skills. Using dangerous drugs will affect a teen's mental capabilities and opportunities for the rest of his or her life.

Teenagers who abuse OxyContin often feel a deep sense of hopelessness and loss of control in their lives.

Out of Control

If a person continues to abuse OxyContin, things can quickly spin out of control. Eventually the body can become dependent on the presence of this drug. When dependency occurs, the constant need for OxyContin will cause even "nice" kids to change to commit terrible acts. Abusing teens may try hard to keep up appearances, but their normal behavior will be interrupted by things they never dreamed they would do.

Many OxyContin abusers trade their lives full of promise for lives of despair.

They may steal money from parents, siblings, or grandparents to pay for pills. The high cost of this habit may force teens to sell prize possessions, such as computers, CD players, video game players, and iPods. They may resort to buying OxyContin on the street from unreliable and dangerous dealers. Furthermore, if a teenager gets caught buying or using OxyContin, he or she could wind up getting probation or even going to jail. As a result of trying OxyContin just one time, many teenagers have ended up with a life that is completely out of control. Some users have described their new OxyContin life as a horrible dream from which they desperately want to wake up.

4
Abusing
OxyContin

Between 2000 and 2001, approximately 558,000 people abused OxyContin for the first time, according to the 2001 National Household Survey on Drug Abuse report. In 2004, the National Survey on Drug Use and Health reported about three million people over the age of twelve have used OxyContin for nonmedical reasons at least once in their lives. An annual survey called Monitoring the Future, funded by the National Institute on Drug Abuse, studies the drug use of young teens in the United States. This survey collects information from approximately 50,000 students each year. The 2006 data revealed 2.6 percent of the students in eighth grade have tried OxyContin at least once in the past year. This number rose significantly from the 1.3 percent of eighth graders that reported using OxyContin in 2002, the first year the survey began collecting OxyContin abuse data. Three percent of the teenagers in tenth grade used OxyContin in 2002. This statistic rose to

The Drug Enforcement Administration (DEA) and the Food and Drug Administration (FDA) spend countless hours trying to protect people from drug traffickers and dishonest Internet pharmacies. These agents raid an illegal pharmaceutical operation in 2005.

3.8 percent in 2006. These increasing numbers show that there is more awareness, acceptance, and popularity of abusing OxyContin among teenagers in recent years. Unfortunately, these students may not know about the increasing number of health problems, deaths, and new cases of drug dependency due to OxyContin abuse.

People who abuse OxyContin often use nicknames such as "OC," "Oxy," "Kicker," and "Oxycotton" to make this potentially deadly drug sound cool, exciting, daring, or even harmless. Abusers also use the terms "40," "80," or "Blue" to describe the particular pills they are selling or using. A catchy, fun name doesn't change what's inside an OxyContin tablet—strong prescription medicine that should only be taken as directed by a doctor.

Why Does Abuse Happen?

Why would people, particularly teenagers, try a dangerous drug like OxyContin? Why has the number of teenage users increased in recent years? Why are young adults willing to die to give OxyContin a try? People in various circumstances have gambled with their health and even their lives by using OxyContin for several different reasons.

Many young adults who live the ugly nightmare of OxyContin abuse say that peer pressure was the reason they first tried the drug. Most teens feel a tremendous need to "fit in." Some believe that going along with a group that is involved in dangerous activities may provide them with an entry into the "cool crowd." The sad truth is, even if a person gains acceptance from a popular group by going along with risky behavior, that person often discovers that this group consists of shallow and immature people who aren't even worth spending time with. Many teens soon realize that people who want you to use dangerous drugs aren't really friends at all. They are usually just confused, insecure people who don't care if they hurt themselves or others.

Sometimes, people face problems that seem too big for them to handle. They often try to escape these problems, rather than work through them. Drug use is one way some people think they can get away from their problems, such as a fight with a sibling, a relationship breakup, a failed exam, or parental expectations that seem unreasonable. Young people may mistakenly believe if they can take something that will help them forget their troubles for a while, these problems will just disappear on their own. Abusing OxyContin won't make problems go away. In fact, using this drug can create new and bigger problems.

Prescription Drugs Are Legal and Safe, Aren't They?

Many teenagers don't think of prescription drugs as potentially harmful. After all, they're manufactured in a clean environment, where workers follow strict quality regulations. They are not mixed or handled by street dealers. Prescription pills are created to help, not hurt. It is this sense of false security that lulls some parents into apathy when it comes to throwing out old prescriptions or keeping close tabs on where they are and who might be using them. It is a mind-set that some teenagers share as well. Most do not believe that the pills their parents use for back pain can harm them or lead to addiction. Teens also find that prescription pills are more socially acceptable than street drugs and are much easier to get. For many young people, they only need to look through the medicine cabinet in the bathroom to find leftover pain pills from a parent's injury or a sister's wisdom tooth surgery.

Life of an Abuser

The life of an OxyContin abuser is full of lies, danger, and despair. Without a constant supply of OxyContin, he or she will become physically ill. Every

Karen Tandy, a DEA administrator, explains in 2005 how one unethical doctor improperly prescribed drugs, including OxyContin, and was sentenced to twenty-five years in prison and fined $1 million for his criminal behavior.

muscle and bone in the body will begin to ache. Nights will be spent tossing and turning in bed, unable to sleep, or lying on the bathroom floor vomiting. When an abuser needs more drugs, he or she may experience extreme cold flashes that feel like the worst case of flu imaginable.

In this miserable state, an abuser usually will try anything to get more of this addictive drug. Some will visit unethical doctors and offer a sizable bribe to get another prescription. They may buy pills from a pharmacist who accepts payments on the side. Others may forge their own prescriptions.

Many OxyContin users go "doctor shopping," or visit many different doctors in the hopes of getting several prescriptions. Any of these risky actions may result in an arrest and a possible trip to jail. But that serious consequence would be better than the alternative—continuing OxyContin abuse and ending up dead.

Signs of an Abuser

What does the life of an OxyContin abuser look like? This person may be angry, irritable, or impatient. His or her behavior will be erratic and unpredictable as this controlling drug takes over. A person who once spent lots of time with friends or playing a favorite sport may lose all interest in these types of activities. An abuser's new best friend, OxyContin, will replace many of the things he or she once found exciting and interesting. The addict will soon lose his or her sense of self and will become like a puppet that reacts to its powerful master, OxyContin.

It's Your
Life

Young people make many decisions that will affect the rest of their lives. Some are more critical and will have a longer-lasting impact than others. Abusing OxyContin is a decision that has ended the hopes and dreams, and even the lives, of many. Ultimately, it's up to you to make wise choices that allow you to have a healthy and bright future. It's your life. Don't throw it away by ignoring the facts and warnings about OxyContin abuse.

Warning Signs

The government created a system to evaluate every drug on the market and share drug safety information with the public. The Food and Drug Administration (FDA) was established to handle this task. This federal agency oversees many things Americans use, such as cosmetics and medical devices, and consume, such as food, dietary supplements, and drugs. The FDA reviews all new drugs before they are approved for medical use.

In 1970, the U.S. Congress passed the Comprehensive Drug Abuse Prevention and Control Act to require drug manufacturers to safeguard and maintain records for particular kinds of drugs. One part of the law, called the Controlled Substances Act, was enacted to help in the fight against drug and substance abuse. The federal government decided to evaluate every drug on the market and place each substance into one of five categories based on how it is to be used, its safety concerns, and its potential for being addictive. The job of enforcing the Controlled Substances Act of 1970 belongs to the Drug Enforcement Administration (DEA). The DEA enforces domestic federal drug laws as well as drug investigations overseas. It is responsible for investigating and preventing people from using controlled substances, such as OxyContin, for non-medical purposes.

Drugs in the first category, Schedule I, are considered to carry the highest risk to the general public. OxyContin is classified as a Schedule II drug, along with drugs such as cocaine, Ritalin, morphine, PCP, and opium. Drugs in this category meet three criteria: they have a high potential for abuse; they have a currently accepted medical use in the United States; and abuse of these drugs may lead to severe psychological or physical dependence. Medical researchers classify OxyContin as a Schedule II drug because it is a highly addictive drug that can put people in grave danger.

DEA personnel help keep the public safe by enforcing all U.S. drug laws and seizing drugs that are being used or sold illegally.

Bottles of OxyContin are marked with a warning label called a black box warning. This is the strongest label that the FDA puts on a prescription drug. Its purpose is to warn patients of the side effects and risks associated with improper use of the drug.

Drugs Don't Discriminate

If you choose to abuse OxyContin, you unleash a powerful amount of oxycodone with unpredictable effects into your body. OxyContin does not discriminate. It doesn't care whose lives it ruins or who it kills. It doesn't know what kind of home you come from or how responsible your parents are. This drug will attack your body no matter what your background. It doesn't care if you're usually a "good" kid and you work hard in school. It won't see that your name is on the honor roll and doesn't even notice that you are a football star. When improperly used, OxyContin has destroyed the

OxyContin Deaths: The Tip of the Iceberg?

The DEA is just beginning to track the growing number of deaths caused by OxyContin abuse in the United States. The DEA asked medical examiners to report the number of OxyContin deaths in 2000 and 2001. The results showed 146 OxyContin "verified" deaths and an additional 318 deaths that were classified as "likely" to have been caused by OxyContin. Because the OxyContin epidemic is relatively new, researchers estimate that hundreds of OxyContin-related deaths every year are never reported.

lives of teenagers and adults all over the country. Anyone can fall victim to this extremely habit-forming prescription medication. If OxyContin users cannot find a way to get new prescriptions or do not have money to buy pills off the street, they may turn to a less expensive drug, such as heroin, to continue getting high. For this reason, OxyContin has been called the gateway to heroin.

A first-time user can become enticed by a drug and slip easily into the habits of a regular abuser. OxyContin is dangerous and deadly for the first-time user and the longtime addict. Abuse and dependency can happen to anyone—even you.

Getting Off OxyContin

People who have fallen into the depths of OxyContin abuse have a long and difficult climb ahead to get out of their pit of dependency—one that often takes months or years.

When a body is suddenly deprived of a drug to which it has become accustomed, it goes through a painful process called withdrawal. OxyContin users experience numerous withdrawal symptoms. Most are so severe that a user will become overwhelmed. No matter how desperately some users want to stop taking OxyContin, many have surrendered to using the drug to avoid the intense suffering that withdrawal brings. Pounding headaches similar to migraines are normal for addicts in withdrawal. Constant vomiting and heavy sweating are also common. Muscle pain can become so severe that the person may be unable to move. Most experience a burning fever followed by chills and cold sweats. Diarrhea, inability to sleep, and leg spasms heap more misery on an addict seeking to break free from OxyContin.

Outside Help

Most recovering OxyContin abusers go to special clinics called rehabilitation centers. Some of these centers are methadone treatment clinics. A methadone clinic dispenses a drug called methadone to patients who are addicted to heroin, OxyContin, and certain other pain medications. This drug helps reduce cravings and withdrawal symptoms. Maintenance therapy is a broader term, which includes giving out other types of medications, such as buprenorphine, for opioid dependency. Both methadone and buprenorphine are opioids and can be abused, but they are given with certain restrictions that try to limit abuse. These centers have trained professionals who can help people deal with the physical and emotional trauma they experience as they try to free themselves from the tight grip of addiction or dependency. A stay at most rehab centers is expensive, but many consider the cost a small price to pay to get their freedom and lives back.

The professionals at a rehabilitation center not only help an addict get through several painful weeks of withdrawal, but they also provide counseling that helps a recovering abuser deal with problems that may have led to his or her drug use in the first place. These specialists help people face issues that their abuse caused, such as broken relationships or problems with the law.

Some users get help while living at home. Many hospitals and clinics offer outpatient treatment for OxyContin abusers. A treatment plan might include a few sessions per week for two to three hours each day. An outpatient program can last from six weeks to a year, depending on the severity of the situation. Treatment choices also include group or individual therapy. In group therapy, patients do not feel alone in their struggle and can learn from others with the same issues. In individual therapy, a person is assigned to a counselor. Counselors suggest activities and provide crucial information about addictive behavior that helps a drug abuser move toward healing and recovery.

Individual counseling assists people in resolving issues that may have led to their having abused OxyContin in the first place. Trained professionals can offer proven methods for a drug user's recovery.

Choices

Everyone has choices, and all choices bring certain consequences. Now that you know the dangers of abusing OxyContin, make the decision ahead of time not to try this dangerous drug. Don't wait until you are suddenly faced with difficult choices or peer pressure to think about this deadly choice. Make up your mind ahead of time to live your life free from the pain and suffering that OxyContin abuse can bring.

Glossary

cerebral cortex The top section of the brain where crucial thinking processes, such as storing and processing language, math skills, and creating strategies, take place.

dependence The state when the body has become accustomed to the presence of a substance and will not function properly without it.

limbic system The section of the brain that is responsible for controlling a person's emotions.

opioid A substance that is produced in the body in order to reduce the sensation of pain; a synthetic substance that creates pain-relieving effects that are similar to those of a natural opioid.

opioid receptor A protein in the body to which opioid drugs attach.

overdose A lethal, or deadly, amount of a drug that can lead to coma or death.

oxycodone A white, odorless powder found in OxyContin pills that helps get rid of pain.

rehabilitation center A live-in facility that offers treatment for addiction.

tolerance When the body becomes less responsive to a drug's effects because of repeated use of the drug.

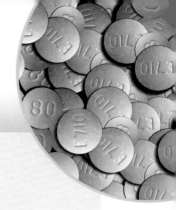

For More Information

American Council for Drug Education

164 West 74th Street

New York, NY 10023

(800) 488-3784

Web site: http://www.acde.org

Canadian Centre on Substance Abuse (CCSA)

75 Albert Street, Suite 300

Ottawa, ON K1P 5E7

(613) 235-4048

Web site: http://www.ccsa.ca

Center for Substance Abuse Treatment (CSAT)

Substance Abuse and Mental Health Services Administration (SAMHSA)

11426-28 Rockville Pike, Suite 410

Rockville, MD 20852

(800) 662-HELP (4357)

Web site: http://www.csat.samhsa.gov

Centre for Addiction and Mental Health (CAMH)

Addiction Assessment

33 Russell Street
Toronto, ON M5S 2S1
(416) 535-8501, ext. 6128
Web site: http://www.camh.net

Community Anti-Drug Coalitions of America
625 Slaters Lane, Suite 300
Alexandria, VA 22314
(800) 54-CADCA (542-2322)
Web site: http://www.cadca.org

Web Sites

Due to the changing nature of Internet links, Rosen Publishing has developed an online list of Web sites related to the subject of this book. This site is updated regularly. Please use this link to access the list:

http://www.rosenlinks.com/idd/oxco

For Further Reading

Aue, Pamela Willwerth. *Teen Drug Abuse*. Farmington Hills, MI: Greenhaven Press, 2006.

Ballard, Carol. *Harmful Substances*. Farmington Hills, MI: The Gale Group, Inc., 2004.

Glass, George. *Drugs and Fitting In*. New York, NY: The Rosen Publishing Group, Inc., 1998.

Haughton, Emma. *Drinking, Smoking, and Other Drugs*. Austin, TX: Raintree Steck-Vaughn Publishers, 2000.

Lockwood, Brad. *OxyContin: From Pain Relief to Addiction* (Drug Abuse and Society). New York, NY: The Rosen Publishing Group, Inc., 2007.

Longnecker, Gesina L. *How Drugs Work: Drug Abuse and the Human Body*. Emeryville, CA: Ziff-Davis Press, 1994.

Olive, M. Foster. *Prescription Pain Relievers* (Drugs: The Straight Facts). Philadelphia, PA: Chelsea House, 2005.

Ramen, Fred. *Prescription Drugs* (Drug Abuse and Society). New York, NY: The Rosen Publishing Group, Inc., 2006.

Rebman, Renee. *Addictions and Risky Behaviors*. San Diego, CA: Lucent Books, 2006.

Roberts, Jeremy. *Prescription Drug Abuse* (The Drug Abuse Prevention Library). New York, NY: The Rosen Publishing Group, Inc., 2000.

Bibliography

"Frontline: Inside the Teenage Brain." Interview: Jay Giedd. Public Broadcasting System. Retrieved November 13, 2006 (http://www.pbs.org/wgbh/pages/frontline/shows/teenbrain/interviews/giedd.html).

National Institute on Drug Abuse. "NIDA InfoFacts: High School and Youth Trends." Retrieved September 18, 2006 (http://www.drugabuse.gov/Infofacts/HSYouthtrends.html).

Office of National Drug Control Policy. "OxyContin." 2006. Retrieved November 7, 2006 (http://www.whitehousedrugpolicy.gov/drugfact/oxycontin/index.html).

The Partnership for a Drug-Free America. "OxyContin." Retrieved September 19, 2006 (www.drugfree.org/Portal/drug_guide/OxyContin).

Pinsky, Drew. *When Painkillers Become Dangerous*. Center City, MN: Hazelden Foundation, 2004.

U.S. Drug Enforcement Administration. "Section 812. Schedules of Controlled Substances." 2002. Retrieved November 5, 2006 (http://www.dea.gov/pubs/csa/812.htm#b).

U.S. Food and Drug Administration. "OxyContin: Questions and Answers." 2001. Retrieved September 18, 2006 (http://www.fda.gov/cder/drug/infopage/oxycontin/oxycontin-qa.htm).

Index

About the Author

Suzanne Slade has written numerous books, often on science topics, for children and young adults. She finds it rewarding to tackle difficult issues that young people face today. She has also written a book for adopted teens, entitled *Adoption, the Ultimate Teen Guide*. Slade lives near Chicago, Illinois, with her husband and two teenage children.

Photo Credits

Cover, p. 1 © www.iStockphoto.com/Bonnie Schupp; p. 8 © Getty Images; pp. 9, 10, 30, 37, 42, 43, 45 © DEA; p. 13 © David Young-Wolff/Photo Edit; p. 17 © Bonnie Kamin/Photo Edit; p. 18 © www.iStockphoto.com/Nancy Louie; p. 21 © Spencer Grant/Photo Edit; p. 22 © Custom Medical Stock Photo; p. 24 © L. Birmingham/ Custom Medical Stock Photo; pp. 27, 33 © AP/Wide World Photos; p. 28 © age footstock/SuperStock; p. 41 © Bill Aron/Photo Edit.

Designer: Les Kanturek; **Editor:** Kathy Campbell
Photo Researcher: Marty Levick